This book belongs to:

~~[crossed out]~~ KAMRYN

Ultimate Princess Treasury

PaRragon

Bath New York Singapore Hong Kong Cologne Delhi Melbourne

First published by Parragon in 2009
Parragon
Queen Street House
4 Queen Street
Bath BA1 1HE, UK

ISBN 978-1-4075-7787-6

Printed in China

Contents

Snow White
and the Seven Dwarfs

Once upon a time, there lived a lovely little princess named Snow White. Her vain and wicked stepmother, the Queen, feared that one day Snow White's beauty would surpass her own. So she dressed the little princess in rags and forced her to work as a servant in the castle.

Each day, the Queen consulted her magic mirror. "Magic Mirror on the wall, who is the fairest one of all?"

As long as the mirror responded in the Queen's favour, Snow White was safe.

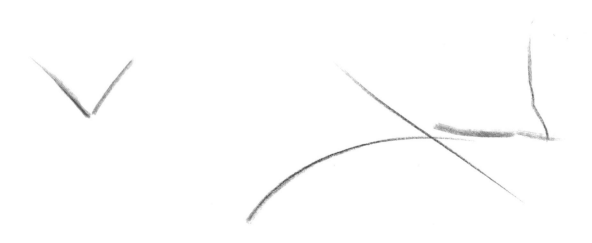

One day, as Snow White was drawing water from a well, she made a wish. She wished that the one she loved would find her, and she dreamed about how nice he would be.

As she gazed into the wishing well, she saw another face reflected in the water. It belonged to a handsome prince. "Hello. Did I frighten you? Please don't run away!"

But the startled princess had fled to her balcony, where she could watch him from afar.

At that moment, the Queen was spying on Snow White and the Prince. When she saw them together, she flew into a jealous rage and rushed to her magic mirror, demanding an answer.

"Famed is thy beauty, Majesty, but hold! A lovely maid I see. Rags cannot hide her gentle grace. She is more fair than thee."

"Alas for her! Reveal her name!"

"Lips red as a rose, hair black as ebony, skin white as snow…"

"SNOW WHITE!"

Furious, the Queen sent for her huntsman. "Take Snow White far into the forest. Find some secluded glade where she can pick wild flowers. And there, my faithful huntsman, you will kill her!"

"But, Your Majesty, the little princess!"

"Silence! You know the penalty if you fail."

Knowing that he dare not disobey the Queen, the huntsman led Snow White into the forest. But when it came time to harm Snow White, he stopped and fell to his knees. "I can't do it. Forgive me, Your Highness!"

"Why, why – I don't understand."

"The Queen is mad! She's jealous of you. She'll stop at nothing. Now quick, child – run, run away. Hide in the woods! Anywhere! And never come back!"

Frightened and alone, Snow White ran into the forest. Blazing eyes peered out at her from the darkness. Eerie shrieks pierced the air. The branches of trees grabbed at her. Finally she could run no further and collapsed to the ground, sobbing.

When Snow White looked up, she saw several forest animals gathered around her.

"Hello. Do you know where I can stay? Maybe in the woods somewhere?"

Snow White followed the animals to a charming little cottage in the woods. She knocked on the door, but no one answered. So she went inside.

"Oh, it's adorable! Just like a doll's house. What a cute little chair. Why, there're seven little chairs. There must be seven little children. And, by the look of this table, seven untidy children. I know – I'll clean the house and surprise them! Then maybe they'll let me stay."

With the help of her animal friends, Snow White cleaned the cottage in no time. Then she decided to check upstairs. "What adorable little beds. And, look – they have names carved on them. Doc, Happy, Sneezy, Dopey… what funny names for children! And there's Grumpy, Bashful and Sleepy. I'm a little sleepy myself." Snow White lay down across three of the tiny beds and fell asleep.

Just then, the owners of the cottage came marching home. They weren't children at all, but seven dwarfs who worked all day in their diamond mine.

As they came into the clearing, the one named Doc made everyone halt. He peered through his glasses. "Look – our house! The lit's light! The light's lit! Door's open. Chimney's smoking. Something's in there!"

The dwarfs peeked inside the cottage. Doc gasped. "Why, the whole place is clean!"

Grumpy, true to his name, crossed his arms and glared. "Mark my words, there's trouble a-brewing. I felt it coming on all day."

Suddenly, the dwarfs thought they heard a sound. Doc looked towards the stairs. "It's up there – in the bedroom."

Cautiously, the seven little men went to investigate. Doc slowly opened the door and peered in. "Why, it's a girl."

As the dwarfs approached the sleeping princess, she began to stir. "She's waking up! Hide!"

Doc dashed behind the beds, and the other dwarfs ran after him.

Snow White yawned and stretched. Then she noticed seven pairs of eyes looking at her over the end of the beds. She sat up, smiling. "How do you do?"

"How do you do what?" Grumpy folded his arms, scowling.

Snow White laughed. "Let me guess. You must be Grumpy."

"Heh! I know who I am. Who are you?"

"Oh – how silly of me! I'm Snow White."

"The princess?" Doc looked very impressed.

But Grumpy frowned. "Tell her to go back to where she belongs."

Snow White pleaded with her hosts. "Please don't send me away! If you do, the Queen will kill me!"

Grumpy shook his head. "The Queen's an old witch. If she finds you here, she'll swoop down and take her vengeance on all of us!"

"Oh, she'll never find me here. And if you let me stay, I'll keep house for you. I'll wash and sew and sweep and cook…"

"Cook!" Doc rubbed his tummy. "Hooray! She stays!"

Back in the castle, the wicked Queen stood before her mirror. "Magic Mirror on the wall, who is now the fairest one of all?"

"Beyond the seventh fall, in the cottage of the seven dwarfs, Snow White still lives, fairest one of all."

"I've been tricked! I'll go myself to the dwarfs' cottage in the woods. I'll go in a disguise so complete, no one will suspect me."

The Queen concocted a magic potion and then transformed herself into an ugly old peddler woman. "And now, a special sort of death for one so fair. What should it be? Ah, a poisoned apple! One taste and Snow White's eyes will close. She will sleep forever, only to be revived by love's first kiss. No fear of that! The dwarfs will think she is dead and bury her alive!"

Back at the cottage, Snow White was saying goodbye to the dwarfs as they set off for work. As she kissed each one on the head, Doc stood close by. "Now, don't forget, my dear, the old Queen's a sly one. Full of witchcraft, so beware."

Grumpy frowned. "Now, I'm warning you – don't let anybody or anything in the house."

Snow White smiled at him, "Why, Grumpy – you do care!"

"Heh!"

Shortly after the dwarfs had left, the old peddler woman appeared at the cottage. "All alone, my pet?" Snow White nodded as the old woman sniffed the air. "Making pies?"

"Yes, gooseberry pies."

"Ah – it's apple pies that make the men-folk's mouths water. Pies made with apples like these." She lifted a shiny red apple from her basket. "Like to try one, dearie? Hmm? Go on – have a bite."

Sensing that Snow White was in danger, several birds swooped down on the woman, knocking the apple out of her hand. Snow White tried to shoo the birds away. "Stop it! Go away! Shame on you, frightening the poor old lady."

"Oh, my heart. Oh, my poor heart. Take me into the house and let me rest. A drink of water, please."

Unable to make Snow White understand,
the birds and animals raced to alert the dwarfs. At
the mine, they pulled and tugged at the confused
little men. Grumpy growled. "What ails these crazy
critters? They aren't acting this way for nothing."

Doc thought about it. " Maybe it's – the
Queen!"

Grumpy galloped off on the back of a deer.
"Snow White's in danger! We've got to save her!"

Meanwhile, the Queen picked up the poisoned
apple. "Because you've been so good to a poor
old woman, I'll share a secret with you. This is no
ordinary apple. It's a magic wishing apple!"

"A wishing apple! Really?"

"Yes. One bite and all your dreams will come
true."

The old woman grinned at the princess. "Perhaps there's someone you love?"

Snow White remembered the prince. "Well, there is someone."

"I thought so. Old Granny knows a young girl's heart. Now, make a wish and take a bite!"

Snow White did so. "Oh, I feel strange."

A moment later, she fell to the ground.

A sudden storm began to rage as the dwarfs reached the cottage, where they found the lifeless Snow White. Through the rain, Grumpy spotted the old hag disappearing into the forest. "There she goes, men. After her!"

The dwarfs chased the Queen up a steep cliff. "You little fools. I'll crush your bones!" She tried desperately to pry a boulder loose to crush them. Suddenly, a bolt of lightning shattered the ledge, sending the wicked Queen into the valley below.

Though the evil Queen was gone forever, the princess was still locked in her spell. So beautiful was she, even in death, that the dwarfs could not find it in their hearts to bury her.

Doc brushed away a tear. "Let's make her a coffin out of glass and gold. That way, we can still see her and keep constant watch by her side."

The Prince heard of the beautiful maiden who slept in the glass coffin. He rode to the cottage of the seven dwarfs and they took him to Snow White. Gently, he kissed her. Then, slowly, her eyes began to open. The spell was broken. Love's first kiss had brought her back to life!

Snow White's wish finally came true. She bid the seven dwarfs goodbye as the handsome prince swept her into his arms. Soon wedding bells rang, echoing throughout the forest. From then on, Snow White and her Prince Charming lived in their castle… happily ever after.

Cinderella

nce upon a time in a small kingdom there lived a beautiful girl called Cinderella. Her mother had died when she was very young and so Cinderella lived alone with her father. She loved her father dearly, but he knew that his daughter needed a mother, so he married again. Cinderella's stepmother had two daughters of her own, Drizella and Anastasia.

Soon, however, Cinderella's father died, leaving his daughter to be cared for by her stepmother. Cinderella soon realised that her new family were jealous of her charm and beauty.

Before long, she was forced to become a servant in her own home. Living in a tiny bedroom in the attic, she only had birds and mice as friends. But through it all, Cinderella still believed her dreams would one day come true.

One morning, Jaq, the little mouse, came running in. A visitor had been caught in a trap! "Hurry, Cinderella! Come-come!" he called.

Cinderella was worried because she really cared for the mice. She always made sure they had enough to eat, and even made little clothes for them to wear. She dashed out of her room and ran down the long stairway to the cellar.

When Cinderella reached the trap, she found a plump little mouse caught inside. Cinderella gave him a little shirt, cap and shoes. She decided to call him Gus.

Cinderella headed for the kitchen to start breakfast. "Don't forget to warn Gus about Lucifer!" she called out to Jaq.

Lucifer belonged to Cinderella's stepmother. He was a sly and lazy cat, and all the other animals hated him, especially Bruno the dog.

After Cinderella had given Lucifer his milk, she went out into the yard.

"It's breakfast time, everybody!" Cinderella called sweetly.

The chickens gathered around Cinderella as she tossed them corn to eat. Major the horse watched happily from the barn.

The mice were invited, too, but first they had to get past Lucifer.

Bravely, Jaq tiptoed silently up behind the nasty cat. With one swift kick, Jaq knocked the cat's paw out from under him and… splat! Lucifer's face fell right into his bowl of milk. Now the mice had time to scurry past Lucifer and out into the yard.

But Gus was so busy gathering food, he didn't notice Lucifer creep up on him until it was too late. At the last minute, Gus managed to escape and scamper up the kitchen table to hide under a teacup.

Just then, a voice shrieked from upstairs. "Cinderella!"

Cinderella's stepmother and stepsisters were impatient for breakfast. Cinderella rushed into the kitchen and grabbed the breakfast trays for the family.   She was in such a hurry, she didn't notice Gus hiding under one of the teacups.

Carefully balancing the trays, Cinderella climbed the long stairway to the bedrooms. As she reached the top of the staircase, she heard a familiar screech. "Cinderella!" It was Drizella.

Cinderella rushed into Drizella's bedroom. "Take that ironing and have it ready in an hour!" Drizella demanded.

Next Cinderella went to Anastasia's room to give her breakfast. "It's about time!" Anastasia whined.

Just as Cinderella left the last tray with her stepmother, she heard a frantic scream. Anastasia had discovered Gus under her teacup! She ran to complain to her mother.

"Come here!" Cinderella's stepmother ordered from the dark shadows of her bed.

Cinderella moved towards the bed and pleaded, "Oh, please, you don't think that I..."

"Hold your tongue!" her stepmother commanded. Assuming Cinderella had put Gus under the teacup on purpose, her stepmother gave her a list of extra chores to do – including giving Lucifer a bath!

Meanwhile, at the royal palace, the King was discussing his son with the Grand Duke. "It's time he got married," said the King. Then he had an idea. "We'll have a ball," he said, "and invite every young maiden in the land. The Prince will surely choose one of them to marry!"

The invitations were sent out that very day.

When the invitation arrived from the palace,
Cinderella took it straight to her stepmother. Drizella
and Anastasia could hardly contain their excitement.
Realising that she, too, was invited, Cinderella
quickly joined in. Her stepsisters laughed at the idea.
But her stepmother said, "I see no reason why you
can't go if you get all your work done and find
something suitable to wear."

Cinderella rushed upstairs to search for the right gown to wear. She chose one that had belonged to her mother. When the mice said that it looked a little old-fashioned, Cinderella smiled. She knew that with a little work, it would be a wonderful new dress.

"Cinderella! Cinderella!" her stepsisters and stepmother called out frantically.

"Oh, now what do they want?" Cinderella sighed, heading for the door.

The mice realised that Cinderella would never have time to finish the dress, so they decided to do it themselves.

Gus and Jaq found a pretty pink sash and a shiny string of blue beads that Cinderella's stepsisters had thrown away. Soon, with a needle and thread, the simple dress was turned into a beautiful gown.

Later that evening, Cinderella climbed wearily up to the attic. Her stepmother and stepsisters had kept her busy right up until it was time to leave for the ball. Now she could only dream about what it would be like to meet the Prince.

Then Cinderella heard something behind her. She turned and saw her new dress.

"Surprise!" called her friends. Cinderella was overwhelmed and thanked her little friends for all their hard work. She dressed quickly and ran down the stairs to join her stepsisters.

But when Drizella and Anastasia saw Cinderella they were filled with jealousy.

"Why, you little thief!" screamed Drizella, tearing at the beads around Cinderella's neck.

Then Anastasia grabbed the sash. "That's mine!" she shrieked, ripping it from the dress. Soon, Cinderella's beautiful gown was in tatters.

Heartbroken, Cinderella ran to the garden in tears. Now her dream would never come true. "There's nothing left to believe in… nothing…" she sobbed.

Then a strange glow appeared in the garden and magical stars shone around Cinderella's head. To her surprise, it was her fairy godmother. Cinderella dried her tears and felt happy at last.

Cinderella's fairy godmother waved her magic wand over a pumpkin. "Bibbidi-bobbidi-boo!" she sang, and the pumpkin became a beautiful coach. Then, before they knew it, Gus, Jaq and two of their friends were turned into four proud white horses. Major became the coachman, and Bruno was transformed into the footman.

With a final wave of her wand, the fairy godmother dressed Cinderella in a magnificent ballgown and sparkling glass slippers.

As Cinderella stepped into her carriage, her fairy godmother gave her a warning. "You only have until midnight," she said. "On the last stroke of twelve the spell will be broken."

The Prince noticed Cinderella the moment she entered the palace. He thought she was the most beautiful girl he had ever seen. Taking her hand in his, he led her to the dance floor.

It seemed as if they had been dancing only minutes when Cinderella heard a clock chime. It was midnight!

"I must go!" cried Cinderella, racing out of the ballroom and down the palace steps. She ran so fast that neither the Prince nor the Grand Duke could catch her, but she lost one of her glass slippers along the way.

Cinderella jumped into her coach just as the Grand Duke found her slipper.

At the last stroke of midnight the coach turned back into a pumpkin and Cinderella found herself dressed in rags once more. Then she noticed she still had a glass slipper. She looked up into the sky with a smile. Hoping her fairy godmother could hear, she whispered, "Thank you for everything!"

The next day, news spread that the Prince was madly in love with the mysterious young woman who had lost her glass slipper. By royal decree, it was decided that the girl whose foot fitted the glass slipper would marry the Prince.

Cinderella's stepmother was determined that either Drizella or Anastasia would be the Prince's bride. She did not want Cinderella to try on the slipper in case it fitted her, so she locked Cinderella in her room just as the Grand Duke and footman arrived at their house.

Anastasia and Drizella took it in turns to try to squash their big feet into the tiny glass slipper. But it was no good. It would just not fit.

"If there are no other ladies in the household, we will bid you good day!" said the footman.

But Jaq and Gus had managed to get the attic key from the stepmother's pocket and free Cinderella from her room. Just as the Grand Duke and footman were about to leave, Cinderella called out from the top of the stairs. "Your Grace! Your Grace! Please wait! May I try on the slipper?"

Cinderella's stepmother demanded that Cinderella not be allowed to try on the glass slipper. The Grand Duke ignored her, but as he approached Cinderella, her stepmother tripped him up with her cane. The slipper flew into the air and shattered on the floor. But Cinderella reached into her pocket and brought out the other glass slipper. The Grand Duke took the slipper and placed it on her foot. It was a perfect fit!

Soon the bells of the palace rang out on Cinderella's wedding day. The King and the Grand Duke smiled as they watched the happy couple get married.

But no one was happier than Cinderella. At last all her dreams had come true, she could live happily ever after without her wicked stepmother, Drizella and Anastasia ruining anything ever again.

Beauty and the Beast

nce upon a time, a young Prince lived in a shining castle. One cold night an old beggar woman arrived, offering him a single rose in return for shelter from the cold. Repulsed by her ugliness, he turned her away. Suddenly she transformed into a beautiful enchantress.

To punish the Prince, she turned him into a hideous beast. Then she gave him a magic mirror and the enchanted rose, telling him it would bloom until his twenty-first year. To break the spell, he must love another and earn that person's love in return before the last petal fell.

Nearby, in a small village, a beautiful young woman named Belle hurried through town. She greeted the townspeople and then rushed to her favourite shop – the bookstore. The owner gave her a book as a gift.

A dreamy look crossed Belle's face. "It's my favourite! Far-off places, daring sword fights, magic spells, a prince in disguise… Oh, thank you very much!"

Belle rushed outside, reading as she walked.

As Belle walked, a handsome hunter named Gaston ran after her. "Belle, the whole town's talking about you. It's not right for a woman to read! It's about time you got your nose out of those books and paid attention to more important things – like me."

Belle tried to get away without being rude, but Gaston's friend LeFou joined them and began to insult her father, an inventor.

"My father's not crazy! He's a genius!" As Belle spoke, an explosion boomed from her father's cottage and she took off running.

At the cottage, Belle found her father and told him what the villagers were saying about her. "They think I'm odd, Papa."

"Don't worry, Belle. My invention's going to change everything for us. We won't have to live in this little town forever!"

Belle's father hitched up their horse, Philippe, and set off for the fair with his new invention. Belle waved. "Good-bye! Good luck!"

But Maurice got lost and accidentally led Philippe into a bleak, misty forest. As he paused to get his bearings, Maurice saw two yellow eyes staring out of the darkness. It was a wolf! Philippe reared and bolted away. Terrified, Maurice ran through the forest with the wolves racing behind him. When he reached a tall, heavy gate, Maurice dashed inside, slamming the gate on the wolves whose sharp teeth snapped at his leg.

Still trembling, Maurice turned to see a huge, forbidding castle. "Hello? I've lost my horse and I need a place to stay for the night."

"Of course, Monsieur! You are welcome here!" Maurice whirled around. There was no one in sight! Then he looked down and saw a mantel clock with a stern, frowning face. Beside him stood a smiling candelabra! Maurice grabbed the clock and examined it. "This is impossible. Why – you're alive!"

The enchantress had also turned all the Prince's servants into household objects. As Cogsworth, the mantel clock, protested, Lumiere, the candelabra, showed Maurice into the drawing room. There he met a friendly teapot named Mrs Potts and her son, a cute teacup named Chip.

Suddenly, the door flew open. A voice boomed, "There's a stranger here…" Maurice jumped out of his chair. In the shadows lurked a large, hulking figure.

"P-P-Please… I needed a place to stay!" Maurice stammered.

"I'll give you a place to stay!" The Beast grabbed Maurice and dragged him out of the room.

Back home at the cottage, Belle heard a knock at the door and opened it. "Gaston! What a 'pleasant' surprise!"

"Belle, there's not a girl in town who wouldn't love to be in your shoes. Do you know why? Because I want to marry you!"

"Gaston, I'm speechless! I'm sorry, but… but… I just don't deserve you." As Gaston left he tripped and fell in the mud. When Belle peeked out, she saw that the villagers had gathered in her yard hoping to see a wedding. The vicar and all Gaston's friends had seen him humiliated!

After the villagers and a very angry Gaston left, Belle ran outside to feed the chickens. There she found Philippe, alone. "Philippe! What are you doing here? Where's Papa?"

The horse whinnied anxiously. Frightened, Belle leaped onto Philippe and returned to the mysterious forest. Soon, they found the castle.

"What is this place?" Belle tried to steady Philippe. Then she saw Maurice's hat on the ground.

Belle hurried inside the gloomy castle and wandered down the vast, deserted corridors.

"Papa? Are you here? It's Belle." No one replied, but Belle didn't know that the Enchanted Objects had seen her.

With joy, Lumiere danced around the mantel clock. "Don't you see? She's the one! She has come to break the spell!"

Finally, Belle discovered Maurice locked in a tower. "Papa! We have to get you out of here!" Suddenly she heard a voice from the shadows.

"What are you doing here?"

Belle gasped. "Please let my father go. Take me instead!"

"You would take his place?"

Belle asked the voice to step into the light and was horrified when she saw the huge, ugly Beast. To save her father, however, Belle agreed to stay in the Beast's castle forever.

The Beast dragged Maurice out of the castle and threw him into a carriage that would return him to town. There, the inventor stumbled into a tavern where Gaston was surrounded by his friends. "Please – I need your help! A horrible beast has Belle locked in a dungeon!"

"Did it have cruel, sharp fangs?" One villager sneered.

Maurice grabbed the man's coat. "Yes! Yes! Will you help me out?"

"We'll help you out, old man." Gaston and his pals tossed the inventor out of the tavern. But Maurice's wild story gave Gaston an idea.

At the castle, Belle nervously followed the Beast upstairs. He paused for a moment. "The castle is your home now, so you can go anywhere you like... except the West Wing."

Belle stared back. "What's in the West Wing?"

"It's forbidden!" Glaring, the Beast opened the door to her room. "You will join me for dinner. That's not a request!"

After the Beast stomped off, Belle flung herself on the bed. "I'll never escape from this prison – or see my father again!"

That night, Belle refused to dine with the Beast. Instead, she crept downstairs to the kitchen. All the Enchanted Objects fed and entertained her. Then Cogsworth agreed to take her on a tour.

Belle halted beneath a darkened staircase. "What's up there?"

"Nothing, absolutely nothing of interest at all in the West Wing."

But when Cogsworth wasn't looking, Belle slipped away and raced up the staircase to a long hallway lined with broken mirrors.

Belle cautiously opened the doors at the end of the corridor and entered a dank, filthy room strewn with broken furniture, torn curtains, and grey, gnawed bones. The only living object was a rose, shimmering beneath a glass dome. Entranced, Belle lifted the cover and reached out to touch one soft, pink petal. She did not hear the Beast enter the room. "I warned you never to come here!" The Beast advanced on Belle. "GET OUT! GET OUT!" Terrified by his rage, she turned and ran.

Belle rushed past Cogsworth and Lumiere as she fled the castle. "Promise or no promise, I can't stay here another minute!"

She found Philippe and they galloped through the snow until they met a pack of fierce, hungry wolves. Terrified, the horse reared and Belle fell to the ground. When Belle tried to defend Philippe, the wolves turned on her, snarling. Suddenly, a large paw pulled the animals off her. It was the Beast!

As Belle struggled to her feet, the wolves turned and attacked the Beast, growling fiercely. With a ferocious howl, the Beast flung off his attackers. As the surprised wolves ran off into the woods, the Beast collapsed, wounded.

Belle knew that this was her chance to escape, but when she looked at the fallen Beast, she could not leave him. "Here, lean against Philippe," she told him, "I'll help you back to the castle."

Meanwhile, Gaston and LeFou were plotting to have Maurice put into Monsieur D'Arque's insane asylum unless Belle agreed to marry Gaston.

At the castle, Belle cleaned the Beast's wounds and thanked him for saving her life. Later, she was quite surprised when he showed her a beautiful library. "I can't believe it! I've never seen so many books in all my life!"

The Beast smiled for the first time. "Then, it's yours!"

That evening Mrs Potts and the other objects watched Belle read a story to the Beast. They were filled with hope that the Beast and Belle were falling in love.

Gradually, the mood in the castle began to change. Belle and the Beast read together, dined together and played together in the snow. They even had a snowball fight! When Belle watched the big awkward Beast try to feed some birds, she realised that he had a kind, gentle side to him – something that she hadn't seen before. In turn, the Beast began to hope that Belle would begin to care for him. He tidied his room, bathed, and dressed up for the evening. He was overjoyed when Belle taught him how to dance.

That evening, the Beast asked Belle if she was happy.

"Yes. I only wish I could see my father. I miss him so much."

"There is a way." The Beast showed Belle the magic mirror. In it, she saw her father lost in the woods, ill from his search for her.

When the Beast saw the unhappy look on Belle's face, he decided to let her go, even if it meant that he would never be human again. Before Belle left, he handed her the magic mirror. "Take it with you so you'll always have a way to look back and remember me."

Heartbroken, the Beast watched as Belle rode off on Philippe. When she found her poor father in the forest, Belle brought him home to their cottage so she could nurse him back to health. But almost as soon as they arrived, a tall, thin man knocked on the door. It was Monsieur D'Arque! He had come to take her father to an insane asylum!

"No, I won't let you!" Belle blocked the way.

LeFou had also convinced the villagers that Maurice was crazy because he was raving like a lunatic about some terrible beast.

Gaston put his arm around Belle. "I can clear up this little misunderstanding – if you marry me. Just say yes."

"I'll never marry you! My father's not crazy. I can prove it!"

Belle showed them the Beast in the magic mirror. "He's not vicious. He's really kind and gentle." Enraged, Gaston shouted, "She's as crazy as the old man! I say we kill the Beast!" The mob of villagers locked Belle and her father in the cellar and stormed the Beast's castle.

As the villagers battled the Enchanted Objects, Gaston forced the Beast onto the castle roof. He clubbed the Beast, who didn't even try to resist. "Get up! Or are you too 'kind and gentle' to fight back?"

"Stop!" Chip had helped Belle and Maurice escape from the cellar. When the Beast saw Belle, he grabbed Gaston by the throat. But his love for Belle had made him too human. He let Gaston go and faced Belle. Without warning, Gaston stabbed the Beast in the back! The Beast roared. Gaston stepped back and tumbled off the roof to his death.

Wounded, the Beast gazed at Belle before he collapsed. She ran to him and held him in her arms. "No! Please! I love you!"

Suddenly, the rain began to shimmer. Slowly, the Beast opened his eyes and in astonishment, he watched his paws transform into hands. He held them out to Belle. "Belle, it's me!"

Belle hesitated and looked into his eyes. "It is you!" The Prince drew her close and kissed her. Then they watched happily as Cogsworth, Lumiere, Chip, Mrs Potts, and all the other servants once again became human. True love had finally broken the spell, and everyone danced for joy.

THE LITTLE MERMAID

nce upon a time, a little mermaid named Ariel frolicked below the ocean, exploring the hulls of sunken ships.

She beckoned to her playmate, a roly-poly fish. "Come on, Flounder! I'm sure this old boat has lots of human treasure aboard."

"I'm not g-g-going in there! It's spooky."

"Don't be such a guppy! Follow me!" Swimming inside the ship's cabin, Ariel discovered some rusted silverware. "Oh, my gosh! Have you ever seen anything so wonderful?"

Ariel swam to the water's surface and found her seagull friend. "Scuttle, do you know what this is?" She held up a fork.

"Judging from my expert knowledge of humans … it's obviously a … a dingelhopper! Humans use these to straighten their hair!"

"Thanks, Scuttle! It's perfect for my collection."

Ariel dove to an undersea grotto, where she kept her treasures from the human world. She hid her collection there because her father, the Sea King, forbade merpeople to have any contact with humans.

That night, Ariel saw strange lights shimmering over the ocean and swam up to investigate.

On the surface, she gaped at fireworks that flared above a large sailing ship. Scuttle soared down through the flickering colours. "Some celebration, huh, sweetie? It's the birthday of the human they call Prince Eric."

Forgetting her father's decree, Ariel peered at the young man on deck. "I've never seen a human this close. He's very handsome."

Aboard the ship, Eric's advisor, Sir Grimsby, motioned for the crew's attention. "It is now my privilege to present our esteemed prince with a very expensive, very large birthday gift – a marble statue carved in his exact likeness! Of course, I had hoped it would be a wedding present."

The prince glanced away, gazing at the sea. "Don't start, Grim. The right girl's out there … somewhere."

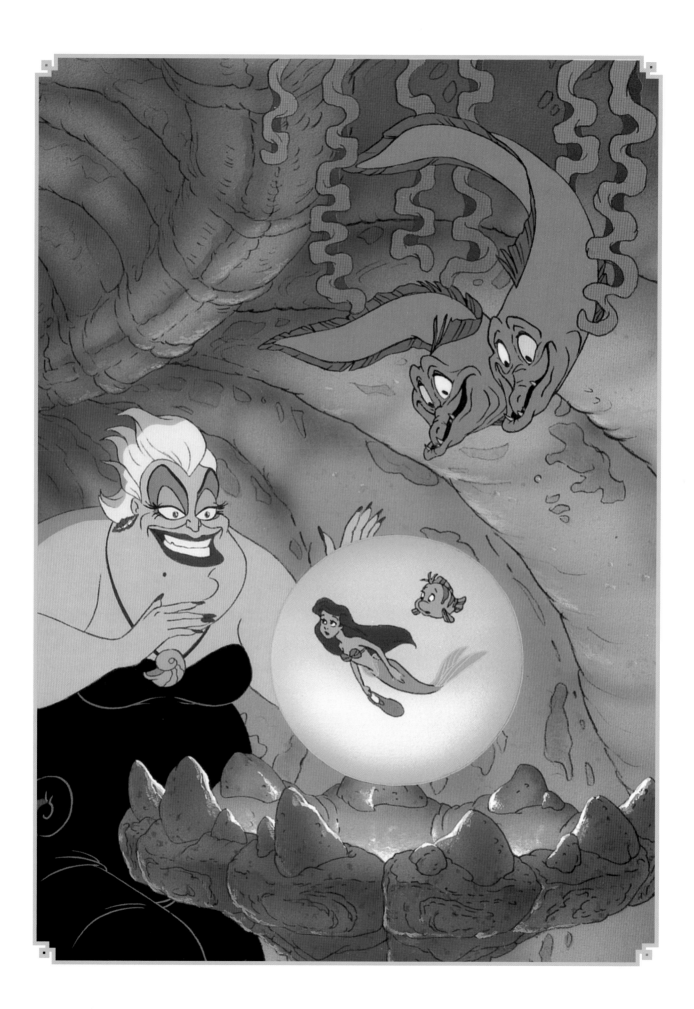

Far beneath the ocean, the wicked Sea Witch, Ursula, used her magic to spy on Ariel. "My, my. The daughter of the great Sea King, Triton, in love with a human! A prince, no less. Her daddy will love that! Serves him right, that miserable old tyrant! Banishing me from his palace, just because I was a little ambitious.

"Still, this headstrong, lovesick girl may be the key to my revenge on Triton. She'll be the perfect bait – when I go fishing for her father!"

On the surface, a sudden storm whipped across the ocean. The prince took charge. "Stand fast! Secure the rigging!"

Without warning, a huge bolt of lightning struck the vessel. Sir Grimsby slid across the deck. "Eric, look out! The mast is falling!"

Ariel watched in horror. "Eric's been knocked into the water! I've got to save him!"

With the storm swirling about her, Ariel desperately searched for Eric. "Where is he? If I don't find him soon – wait, there he is!"

Diving beneath the waves, Ariel spotted the unconscious figure. "He's sinking fast! I've got to pull him out of the water before he drowns!" She took hold of Eric and, using all her strength, managed to drag him to the surface.

As the storm died down, Ariel dragged the unconscious prince to shore. "He's still breathing! He must be alive."

A Jamaican crab scuttled across the sand. It was Sebastian, the Sea King's music director. "Ariel, get away from that human! Your father forbids contact with them, remember?"

"But Sebastian, why can't I stay with him? Why can't I be part of his world?" And she sang a haunting melody that voiced her longing to be with Eric forever.

A moment later, Ariel was back in the water, and Sir Grimsby was kneeling beside Eric. "You really delight in these sadistic strains on my blood pressure, don't you?"

"Grim, a girl rescued me… She was singing in the most beautiful voice…"

"I think you've swallowed a bit too much seawater! Here, Eric, let me help you to your feet."

Back at the coral palace, Triton noticed Ariel floating about as if in a dream. Summoning Sebastian, the Sea King smiled. "You've been keeping something from me. I can tell Ariel's in love."

"I tried to stop her! I told her to stay away from humans!"

"Humans! Ariel is in love with a human?"

Triton found Ariel in her grotto. She was staring at Eric's statue, which Flounder had retrieved after the storm. "How many times have I told you to stay away from those fish-eating barbarians! Humans are dangerous!"

"But, Daddy, I love Eric!"

"So help me, Ariel, I am going to get through to you no matter what it takes!" Raising his trident, the Sea King destroyed all her treasures. Then he stormed off, leaving Ariel in tears.

As she wept, two eels slithered up to her. "Don't be ssscared. We represent sssomeone who can help you!"

Ariel followed them to Ursula's den. "My dear, sweet child! I haven't seen you since your father banished me from his court! To show that I've reformed, I'll grant you three days as a human to win your prince. Before sunset on the third day, you must get him to kiss you. If you do, he's yours forever. But if you don't – you'll be mine!"

Ariel took a deep breath and nodded. The Sea Witch smiled deviously. "Oh yes, I almost forgot. We haven't discussed payment. I'm not asking much. All I want is – your voice!"

Sebastian, who had followed Ariel, scurried out of hiding. "Don't listen, Ariel! She is a demon!" But Ursula had already used her powers to capture Ariel's beautiful voice in a seashell – and transform the little mermaid into a human!

Aided by Sebastian and Flounder, Ariel used her new legs to swim awkwardly to shore. There she found Prince Eric walking his dog. "Down, Max, down! I'm awfully sorry, miss."

Eric studied Ariel as she shied away from the animal. "Hey, wait a minute. Don't I know you? Have... have we ever met?"

Ariel opened her mouth to answer, forgetting that her voice was gone. The prince lowered his eyes.

"You can't speak or sing, either? Then I guess we haven't met."

Eric gently took Ariel's arm. "Well, the least I can do is make amends for my dog's bad manners. C'mon, I'll take you to the palace and get you cleaned up."

At the royal estate, Ariel was whisked upstairs by a maid. Grimsby discovered the prince staring glumly out the window. "Eric, be reasonable! Young ladies don't go around rescuing people, then disappearing into thin air!"

"I'm telling you, she was real! If only I could find her…"

The following afternoon, Eric took Ariel for a rowboat ride across a lagoon. Sebastian swam below them. "Almost two days gone and that boy hasn't puckered up once! How she gonna get that boy to kiss her? Maybe this will help create the romantic mood."

He began conducting a sea-creature chorus. "C'mon and kiss the girl… The music's working! Eric's leaning over to kiss Ariel." But as the prince bent toward her, the boat tipped and both Eric and Ariel fell into the water!

From her ocean lair, Ursula saw them tumble into the lagoon. "That was too close for comfort! I can't let Ariel get away that easily!"

She began concocting a magic potion. "Soon Triton's daughter will be mine! Then I'll make the Sea King writhe and wriggle like a worm on a hook!"

The next morning, Scuttle flew into Ariel's room to congratulate her. The prince had announced his wedding!

Overjoyed at the news, Ariel hurried downstairs. She hid when she saw Eric introducing Grimsby to a mysterious dark-haired maiden. The prince seemed hypnotized. "Vanessa saved my life," he said. "We're going to be married on board ship at sunset."

Ariel drew back, confused. She was the one who had rescued Eric! Fighting tears, she fled the palace. Sebastian found Ariel sitting on the dock, watching the wedding ship leave the harbour.

Suddenly, Scuttle crash-landed beside them. "When I flew over the boat, I saw Vanessa's reflection in a mirror! She's the Sea Witch – in disguise! And she's wearing the seashell containing Ariel's voice. We've got to stop the wedding!"

Sebastian splashed into the water. "Flounder, you help Ariel swim out to that boat! I'm going to get the Sea King!"

Dripping wet, Ariel climbed aboard the ship just before sunset, as Eric and the maiden were about to be married. Before Vanessa could say "I do", Scuttle and an army of his friends attacked her. In the scuffle, the maiden's seashell necklace crashed to the deck, freeing Ariel's voice. Suddenly, Vanessa sounded like the Sea Witch. "Eric, get away from her!"

Ariel smiled at the prince. "Oh Eric, I wanted to tell you …"

Ursula grinned. "You're too late! The sun has set!"

Ariel felt her body changing back into a mermaid. As she dove into the water, the witch transformed her into a helpless sea plant. "You're mine, angelfish! But don't worry – you're merely the bait to catch your father! Why, here he is now!"

"I'll make a deal with you, Ursula – just don't harm my daughter!"

Instantly, Triton was changed into a tiny plant, and Ariel resumed her mermaid form. She stood heartbroken before Ursula, now Queen of the Ocean.

Suddenly, Prince Eric appeared. He tossed a harpoon at the Sea Witch, hitting her in the arm. Ursula snatched up the king's trident. "You little fool!"

As the Sea Witch pointed the weapon at Eric, Ariel rammed into her, knocking the trident loose. "Eric, we have to get away from here!"

The moment they surfaced, huge tentacles shot out of the ocean. "Eric, we're surrounded. Look out!" Ariel gasped as an enormous monster emerged. It was the Sea Witch! Using her new powers, the witch commanded the waters into a deadly whirlpool. Several old sunken ships rose to the surface. The prince struggled aboard one of the boats. As Ursula loomed above Ariel, Eric plunged the sharp prow through the Sea Witch, destroying her. The mighty force sent Eric reeling toward shore.

As the unconscious prince lay on the beach, Ariel perched on a rock and gazed at him. Triton and Sebastian watched from afar. "She really does love him, doesn't she, Sebastian?"

The Sea King waved his trident, and Ariel was once again human.

The next day, she and Prince Eric were married on board the wedding ship. As they kissed, the humans and merpeople sent up a happy cheer, linked at last by the marriage of two people whose love was as deep as the sea and as pure as a young girl's voice.

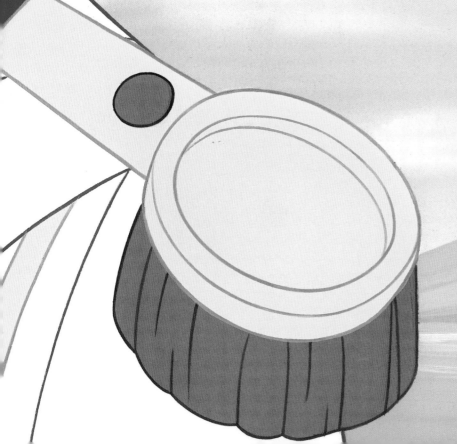

Sleeping Beauty

ong ago, in a far away land, King Stefan and his Queen held a feast to celebrate the birth of their daughter, Aurora. King Hubert and his young son, Phillip, came from a neighbouring kingdom to attend the feast.

The two kings made plans for Phillip and Aurora to marry on the Princess's sixteenth birthday.

Also at the celebrations were the princess's three fairy godmothers, Flora, Fauna and Merryweather. Each of them had a special gift for the Princess.

First, Flora waved her magic wand over the baby's cradle and said, "I give you the gift of beauty."

Then, Fauna waved her wand and said, "I give you the gift of song."

Finally, Merryweather fluttered over to the cradle. She raised her wand to grant the third gift, when…

Suddenly, there was a crack of lightning. Maleficent, the wicked fairy, stormed in. She was furious that she had not been invited to the celebrations.

Stroking her pet raven, Maleficent glared at the baby Princess. "I also have a gift for you," she hissed. "Before the sun sets on your sixteenth birthday, you will prick your finger on the spindle of a spinning wheel and die!"

Maleficent threw back her head and laughed wickedly. Then, she disappeared in a cloud of purple smoke.

Merryweather gave a gentle cough. "I still have my gift for the Princess," she reminded the horrified King and Queen.

She went over to the cradle and whispered, "When the spindle pricks your finger, you will not die. Instead, you will fall into a deep, enchanted sleep. From this slumber you shall wake when true love's kiss the spell shall break."

The King was still terribly worried about his daughter's safety. He ordered every spinning wheel in the kingdom to be burned. Then, he and the Queen sadly agreed to the fairy godmothers' plan. They took Aurora far away to a place where Maleficent wouldn't be able to find her until her sixteenth birthday had passed.

Flora, Fauna and Merryweather renamed the Princess Briar Rose. They moved into a little cottage in the woods. There, the fairies put away their magic wands and disguised themselves as simple peasant women.

As the years passed, Maleficent kept searching for the Princess, but she never found her.

As the Princess's sixteenth birthday drew nearer, Maleficent sent her trusted pet raven to try and find her. It was Maleficent's last chance.

The morning of Briar Rose's birthday finally arrived. The three fairies sent her to collect berries in the woods, while they prepared some birthday surprises.

After gathering the berries, Briar Rose rested in a woodland glade. She sang about falling in love with a handsome prince.

Her woodland friends found a cloak, a hat and a pair of boots that had been left in the forest. They dressed up as a make-believe prince. Briar Rose joined in their game, dancing and singing with them.

The clothes belonged to Prince Phillip, who, after a long ride, was resting in the woods with his horse. Phillip was enchanted by the beautiful singing coming through the trees and went to see who it was.

The moment they met, Briar Rose and the handsome stranger fell in love. They felt sure that they
had met somewhere before. When it was time for Briar Rose to leave, they arranged to meet that evening at the cottage in the woods.

Meanwhile, the three fairies set about making their birthday surprises. But before long they were in a terrible muddle! Fauna had baked a birthday cake. But the mixture was too runny and the cake was lopsided!
Flora and Merryweather had made a special gown for Briar Rose, but it was an awfully funny shape!

"It's no use," said Merryweather. "We need to use magic to sort this out. I'll fetch the wands."

Before they dared to use their wands, the fairies blocked up every gap in the cottage. They had to stop any magic dust from escaping and alerting Maleficent to their hideaway. But they forgot to block the chimney!

It was so wonderful to be able to use magic again! Flora waved her wand and a beautiful pink gown appeared.

Then Merryweather waved her wand and changed the gown to blue. Flora changed it back to pink. All the time, magic dust was escaping from the chimney.

Maleficent's raven was searching nearby. He saw the magic dust and decided to fly down and investigate.

When Briar Rose returned to the cottage she thanked her fairy godmothers for the beautiful new gown and the delicious cake.

"This is the happiest day of my life," she said. Then she told them about the handsome stranger she had met in the woods. He planned to visit her at the cottage that very evening.

"It's time we told Briar Rose the truth," said Fauna.

So, Briar Rose learnt that she was really a princess and would soon have to marry Prince Phillip.

"Today you must return to the palace and start your new life," said Flora.

Up on the chimney, Maleficent's raven smiled.

Briar Rose was heartbroken. She didn't want to marry a prince. She had fallen in love with the handsome stranger she had met in the woods.

By now, the raven had heard enough. He flew off to tell his mistress that the search for Princess Aurora was over.

As soon as darkness fell, the fairy godmothers led Briar Rose through the forest to the palace. They had no idea that Maleficent was already there, lying in wait for them.

At the palace, the fairy godmothers left Aurora in a quiet room to rest. Suddenly, a strange glowing light appeared. Aurora followed it in a trance. It led her up a winding staircase to an attic room.

Inside the room Maleficent was waiting by a spinning wheel. Aurora had never seen a spinning wheel before. The wicked fairy urged the princess to touch it. Aurora reached out and pricked her finger on the spindle. In an instant she had fallen into a deep sleep.

Before long, the fairy godmothers found Aurora lying by the spinning wheel. They quickly cast a sleeping spell over the entire palace.

Luckily, the fairies had discovered that Prince Phillip was the stranger with whom Briar Rose had fallen in love. Only his kiss could wake her! So, while everyone was asleep, the fairies thought of a plan. They would return to the cottage, find Phillip and bring him back to the palace.

But they were too late! Maleficent and her soldiers had already found the Prince waiting at the cottage and captured him.

Maleficent took Phillip back to her castle where she threw him into her deepest, darkest dungeon. She fastened him to the wall with chains and left him there to die.

When the fairies couldn't find Prince Phillip at the cottage, they soon realized Maleficent must have captured him. They quickly made their way to her castle.

As soon as it was safe, the fairies magically appeared in the dungeon and freed the prince. They waved their wands and armed him with a magic shield of virtue and a gleaming sword of truth.

Then, the Prince jumped on his horse and galloped off to King Stefan's palace to rescue Princess Aurora.

When Maleficent discovered that the Prince had escaped she roared with rage. She cast a spell that surrounded the palace with a forest of thorns. But Phillip was able to cut his way through with his magic sword.

Suddenly, a huge and terrible black dragon appeared. The dragon laughed wickedly – it was Maleficent! Prince Phillip held up his magic shield so that the scorching flames could not harm him.

The battle had begun! The dragon soared into the air and swooped down towards Prince Phillip. The Prince hurled his magic sword at the dragon's chest. The beast crashed to the ground. Maleficent was dead!

Prince Phillip raced towards the palace. He quickly found the room where Sleeping Beauty lay. As he gently kissed her, she opened her eyes – the spell was broken!

The fairy godmothers' spell was broken too. All round the palace, people began to wake from their enchanted sleep.

The King and Queen were delighted to have their beloved daughter back again. That evening, a magnificent ball was held to celebrate the wedding of Phillip and Aurora. The Princess was dressed in the beautiful blue gown, but Flora couldn't resist turning the blue gown back to pink. Then Merryweather turned it back to blue and so it went on, pink… blue…pink…

The Princess danced happily in the arms of her Prince, while their proud fathers looked on.

A dream come true, the Prince and Princess lived happily ever after.

The End